"Once upon a time . . . there was the simple understanding that to sing at dawn and to sing at dusk was to heal the world through joy. The birds still remember what we have forgotten, that the world is meant to be celebrated."

Terry Tempest Williams

For anyone who needs a friend like Moth

an imprint of Candlewick Press

The Circles in the Sky

Karl James Mountford

Fox ignored the bright light from the
big circle in the sky and nestled down
in his den after a night of hunting.

He couldn't settle, though, because
of the loud chorus of noise outside.
It was those birds, singing
for all to hear.

But this song was not like their usual song.
It was neither happy nor sad . . . it was different.

Fox tramped out of his den and followed
the strange morning song.

He traveled across
the rushing river . . .

past the forgotten house . . .

and through the woods,
which had more stumps than tall tree trunks.
Before Fox knew it, the day had become
a lot older. When suddenly . . .

the song ended, and Fox came to a halt.
The birdsong had led him to a place
where all kinds of flowers grew.

Fox couldn't remember having been
to a place like this before.

Distracted by his surroundings,
Fox almost didn't notice
the huddle of birds, until
they burst into flight,
as birds often do.

And there, in the clearing, was something small,
something still . . . perhaps forgotten.

It was just a bird.
Fox moved closer and closer, but Bird
didn't move. Not a little. Not a bit.

Fox tried scaring Bird, but Bird
didn't frighten. He found a worm
for Bird to eat, but Bird didn't bite.
Fox tried singing, but Bird didn't join in.

Nothing seemed to work.
Nothing seemed to help.
Fox couldn't understand why.
What could he do for
the broken bird?

Unbeknownst to Fox,
a lofty moth had been watching
for some time. Moth was
curious about the odd fox.

"Bird doesn't need fixing, Fox. Bird just isn't *here* anymore," said Moth kindly.

"What do you mean, Moth?
Bird's right here, all bird-shaped."
Fox gestured.

"Well, sometimes there can be a different kind of *here*. Bird's not here anymore in the way you and I are."

"You make no sense, Moth."

"Oh," said Moth, shrinking back.

Neither creature spoke for
a little while; they just sat
in the quiet with the bird.

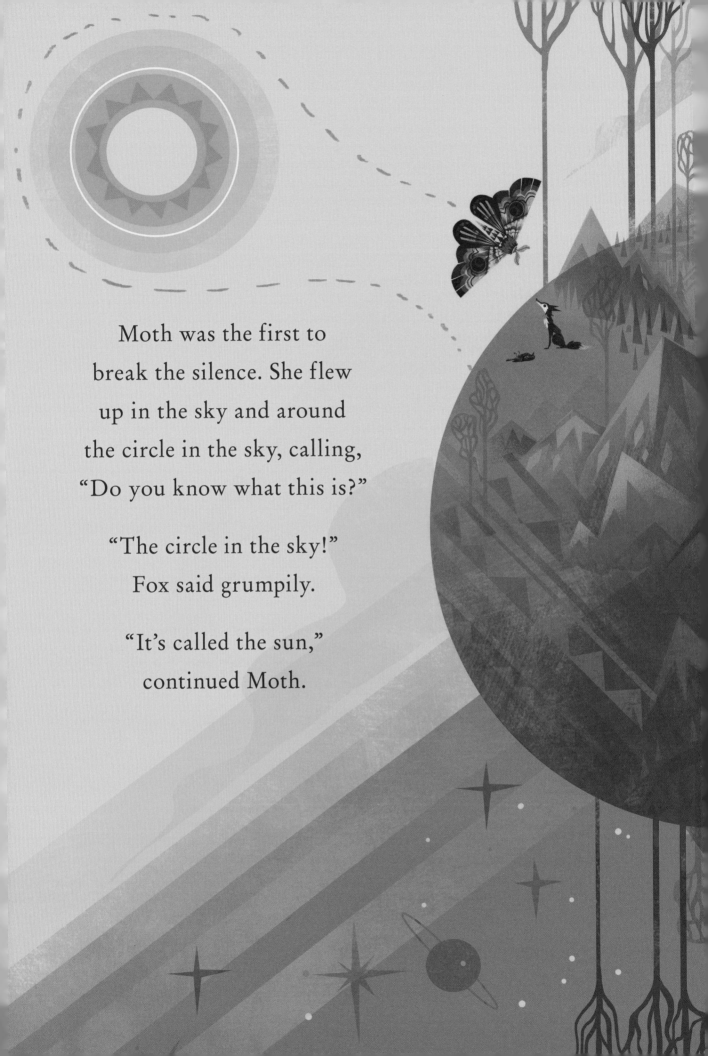

Moth was the first to
break the silence. She flew
up in the sky and around
the circle in the sky, calling,
"Do you know what this is?"

"The circle in the sky!"
Fox said grumpily.

"It's called the sun,"
continued Moth.

"When the sun goes down
and the moon rises, the sun isn't
here anymore. But because the sun
is so bright, her light—even on the
darkest of nights and no matter
how far away—is reflected
in the moon.

"So even if the moon can't see
or be with the sun, he never
forgets that she was once here."

"But the sun rises
again in the
morning, Moth.
Are you saying Bird
will be back tomorrow?!"
Fox said hopefully.

"No, Fox. Bird's not a sun
or a moon . . . it's just—"
But before Moth could
finish her sentence . . .

Fox howled,
"YOU'RE STILL
NOT MAKING SENSE.
STOP TALKING ABOUT
MOONS AND SUNS.
JUST TELL ME THE TRUTH.
IF BIRD IS NOT HERE,
WHERE IS BIRD?"

"I was trying to
be kind," said Moth.
"Sad things are hard to hear.
They are pretty hard to say, too.
They should be told in little pieces.

"Bird isn't here anymore . . .
because . . . Bird is dead."

Fox didn't know that word well,
but he felt it. He tried to
hold this strange feeling back.

"It's OK to be sad," comforted Moth.
And with that said, a few tears escaped
Fox's eyes, and he let them fall.

The two creatures sat down in grief
for some time.

"I don't know why I cried; I barely know Bird,"
said Fox. "It's just all so . . ."
"So very sad," helped Moth.

"I think I understand what you were saying earlier,
Moth, about the circles in the sky.
Even if they can't be together,
the moon will always remember the sun.

That's what I can do
for Bird, right?
I can remember him."

"It's all we can do,"
Moth reassured Fox.

"It's nice,
Moth—that way
of thinking," said Fox.

"I like to think so, but I'm
just a moth. A rabbit or an owl
might believe something different."

"What do we do
now, Moth?" said Fox.
"I can't just leave Bird out here
all alone."

"Bird will never be alone.
The circles in the sky will watch over him.
As for you, it's been quite a day, hasn't it?
Perhaps it's time for home," said Moth.

"Home seems so far away from here." Fox sighed.

"If you want, I could keep you
company on the journey,"
Moth offered.
"We just have one last thing to
do before we start the long
walk back."

Fox and Moth set Bird among
the wildflowers and said
a last goodbye.

They strolled through the
cut-down woodland that had
space for something new to grow.

Past the forgotten house,
that was probably really
loved once.

And across the calm river
that made soothing sounds.

Rather than walk alone,
the two creatures had each other for
company. And as the dawn began to break . . .

the birds were singing
for a brave new day.